KATHLEEN LEVERICH

HILARY
and the
TROUBLEMAKERS

Illustrated by Walter Lorraine

A Beech Tree Paperback Book
NEW YORK

The Library of Congress has cataloged the Greenwillow Books edition of
Hilary and the Troublemakers as follows:
Hilary and the troublemakers / by Kathleen Leverich;
pictures by Walter Lorraine.
p. cm.
Summary: A homework-eating owl, an angry piggy back, several talking
sheep, and some snow people help Hilary to make the right decisions at
home and at school.
ISBN 0-688-10857-1
[1. Imagination—Fiction. 2. Conduct of life—Fiction.]
I. Lorraine, Walter, ill. II. Title. PZ7.L5744Hi 1992
[Fic]—dc20 91-13762 CIP AC

10 9 8 7 6 5 4 3 2 1
First Beech Tree Edition, 1999
ISBN 0-688-16453-6

FOR NANCY, MY MOTHER

Contents

Owl Food

Time after time, mysterious characters got Hilary Hummer into trouble. These pests never bothered Mr. and Mrs. Hummer. They never bothered Hilary's big sister, Angelica, or her big brother, Jack. They waited until Hilary was alone and then they bothered her.

One brisk September morning Hilary was on her way to school when a giant owl stepped out of the bushes and stopped her.

"I'm hungry," said the owl. "Give me your

homework to eat." The owl had fierce yellow
eyes, powerful claws, and a dangerous-looking
beak. It was twice as tall as Hilary and smelled like
a pile of old clothes.

Hilary hugged her notebook and backed up a
step. "I didn't know that owls ate homework."

The bird stepped closer. "This owl does. Hand
yours over, or else!"

That *or else* sounded serious. Hilary opened her
notebook. She took out her homework paper, but

slowly. "These are fractions," she said. She hoped the owl wouldn't want to eat fractions. They had taken hours and hours of hard work—

"Fractions!" The owl reached out a powerful claw and snatched the paper from her hands. "Fraction homework is my special favorite!"

In one loud gulp, Hilary's homework paper disappeared.

"Very tasty." The owl licked its beak and spread its wings. With an odor of old clothes, it flapped away.

At school that morning Mr. Caruso said, "Everyone pass your homework paper to the front."

Jared passed his. Dean passed his. Emily passed hers—

"Hilary?" said Mr. Caruso.

Hilary's cheeks got hot. "A giant owl took my homework."

"A giant owl?" said Mr. Caruso.

Hilary coughed. She straightened her glasses. "He ate it."

Russell covered his mouth and snickered.

Bonnie laughed so hard her shoulders shook.

Mr. Caruso turned to the rest of the class, "Was anyone else troubled by this homework-eating bird?"

Jared shook his head.

Emily shook hers.

Everyone else said, "No-ooh!"

Mr. Caruso nodded thoughtfully. He went to the blackboard and wrote "HIL—"

Hilary knew what was coming.

"—ARY."

So did everyone else.

Mr. Caruso put down the chalk, dusted his hands, and turned to Hilary. "You may make up the assignment after school. I'll see that no giant owl bothers you."

That evening at dinner Mr. Hummer said, "Hilary, you're very quiet. Did something happen today at school?"

"Wel-ll—" Hilary straightened her glasses and told her family the whole story.

"Giant *owl*?" Jack burst out laughing.

Angelica said, "If you hadn't done your homework, you should have told Mr. Caruso the truth."

"I did my homework! I told the truth!" Hilary hated it when Angelica and Jack ganged up on her. She hated it when they talked to her the way grown-ups would.

Mr. Hummer frowned. "We'd like to believe you, but it's an awfully tall story."

"It's an awfully tall *owl!*" said Hilary. "And fierce. It said, 'Give me your homework, or else!'"

"Or else, what?" said Angelica.

Jack speared a french fry. "Maybe, this bird only looks big to you because you're so little."

That was what Hilary hated most of all: having Angelica and Jack treat her like a baby. Having them laugh at her and call her little, and now that they were both in junior high school, they were always doing it! They left Hilary behind to go places with friends. They laughed together at private jokes and when she said, "What's so funny?" wouldn't share them. When the three of them were younger, they used to play together all the time. But now if she asked to join their games, they said, "You're too little. Why don't you make up games you can play by yourself? When we were your age, that's what we did."

"You and Angelica always act so big!" said Hilary.

Jack looked at Angelica.

Angelica crunched a roll and shrugged. "If Jack and I act big, Hilary, it's because *big* is what we are."

"Angelica! Jack! That's enough," said Mrs. Hummer. "I'm sure Hilary has seen the last of that giant pigeon."

"Owl," said Jack. "It was a giant *owl*."

"Never mind!" said Mr. Hummer. He turned to Hilary. "You won't be meeting any more homework-eating birds, will you?"

Hilary remembered the owl's fierce yellow eyes.

She remembered its powerful claws and its serious-looking beak. "I certainly hope not!"

Mr. Hummer broke his dinner roll in two. "Very well. See that you don't!"

The next morning Hilary was on her way to school when the giant owl stepped out of the bushes and stopped her.

"I'm hungry," said the owl. "Give me homework to eat."

Hilary clutched her notebook and shook her head. "I gave you my homework yesterday, and I got into trouble. I won't give you any homework today."

The owl blinked its yellow eyes. It flexed its powerful claws and snapped its dangerous beak. It looked Hilary up and down. "Very well, give me your wristwatch. I'll eat that."

Hilary looked at her watch. Mr. and Mrs. Hummer had given it to her for her birthday. With its round face and black painted numerals, it wasn't at all the kind of watch Hilary wanted. She'd wanted a watch with numerals that flashed and buttons that pushed and alarms that beeped and buzzed. Still, it had been thoughtful of her parents to buy it for her.

"Well?" The owl raised its wings until it hovered over Hilary like a dangerous storm.

Hilary unfastened the watch strap from her wrist. She handed the watch to the owl. "This is the last time I'll let you pick on me. From now on, leave me alone!"

The owl couldn't answer with its beak full of wristwatch. Instead, it gave Hilary a nasty wink and flapped away.

At dinner that evening Mr. Hummer said, "What happened at school today, Hilary?"

"Wel—ll—" Hilary straightened her glasses. "In the morning we had a spelling bee. After lunch I did an experiment for my science project—"

"Did you hand in your homework?" said Angelica.

Hilary frowned, "If it's any of your business, handing in homework was the first thing I did."

"Well done!" said Mr. Hummer. "Your mother

and I knew we could count on you. Didn't we, dear?"

Mrs. Hummer didn't answer. She wasn't looking at Mr. Hummer. She wasn't paying attention to what he said. She was staring, instead, at a bare spot on Hilary's left wrist. "Hilary," she said finally. "Where is your very expensive birthday watch?"

Hilary didn't get any dessert that evening. She didn't get to watch her favorite TV program. Instead, Mrs. Hummer gave her a sharp scolding about telling the truth. While Angelica and Jack snickered, Mr. Hummer sent her to her room.

"No one ever believes me!" Hilary slammed her door and sat down hard on her bed.

"Nfftt-nfftt-nfffft." From her cage across the room Hilary's gerbil, Clover, sniffed in a sympathetic way.

"Tomorrow morning that owl's sure to stop me," said Hilary. "What will I do then?"

"Chuukaa-chuukaa-chuukaa," chattered Clover.

"What would you do if a giant owl picked on you?" said Hilary.

Clover scurried around her gerbil tumble wheel so fast, she made the bell ring, *Dnngg-dnngg-dnngg!*

"Thank you for the suggestion," said Hilary. "But running away won't work. That owl would snatch me in its powerful-looking claws before I took two steps." She offered Clover a carrot. "I'll have to think of some other plan."

The next morning Hilary took a different route to school. This roundabout way was much longer and very hilly. Hilary was out of breath and hurrying when the giant owl stepped out of the bushes and stopped her.

"Oh, no!" said Hilary.

The owl stepped closer. "That wristwatch you gave me yesterday was tasty. I'd like another."

"Pest!" cried Hilary. "Last night I missed dessert. I missed my favorite TV program. I let you eat my birthday watch, and because of that, I spent the whole evening in my room."

The owl yawned. "If you have no more wristwatches, give me homework to eat."

Hilary hid her notebook behind her back.

The owl stepped closer and pointed a wing. "Your red spectacles look tasty. I'll take them."

Hilary dropped her notebook and clamped her hands to the sides of her glasses. "Without glasses, I can't see!"

"Spectacles or homework," said the owl. "Homework or spectacles!"

"Nasty bird!" Hilary kept one hand firmly on her glasses as she knelt beside her notebook. She kept her hand on her glasses as she opened the notebook and took out her homework paper.

"Fractions?" said the owl hopefully.

Hilary shook her head. "State capitals. I'm going to get into lots of trouble—"

"State capitals can be tasty." The owl snatched the homework in its beak and flapped away.

By the time Hilary got to school, the playground was empty. There was not a single person in the halls, and every classroom door was firmly shut.

I must be late, thought Hilary. She hurried on tiptoe down the long hallway. She couldn't be sure how late. Thanks to the giant owl, she had no wristwatch to tell her the time.

She reached her classroom and put her hand on the knob. Cautiously, she opened the door.

"Hilary, how good of you to join us," said Mr. Caruso. "Class, aren't we pleased that Hilary decided to drop in?"

Emily and Dean snickered.

John and Tanasha covered their mouths and laughed.

Mr. Caruso turned to look at the classroom clock. "Can you tell us why you're arriving half an hour late?"

"Wel–ll," said Hilary. Everyone was looking at her. Everyone was waiting to hear what she'd say. "I *could* tell you, but you wouldn't like it."

"Let me guess," said Mr. Caruso. "Does it have fierce yellow eyes, huge wings, and the habit of eating your homework?"

Hilary said, "It has all those things. Plus the habit of trying to steal my glasses!"

"That greedy bird!" said Mr. Caruso. "How did you stop it?"

Hilary looked at her classmates. Twenty-seven faces looked back. "I gave that owl something else."

Mr. Caruso raised his eyebrows. "Something else? What something?"

Hilary studied her shoes. "I gave that owl my state capitals homework."

Jared snickered.

So did Emily.

Ben and the rest of the class did, too.

"Since everyone finds owls so interesting," said Mr. Caruso. "Each of you may prepare a report tonight on that subject."

Everyone groaned. "Do we have to?"

Mr. Caruso fixed Hilary with a stern look. "See me after school, young lady. I'll have a note for you to take home."

"Owls again!" said Mr. Hummer when he read the note that evening.

Hilary shook her head. "Not *owls*. One giant owl who's fierce and says *or else!*"

Angelica giggled, "Hoot-hoot, I'm the giant owl. Give me fractions to eat!"

Jack joined in, "Give me tasty gerbils named Clover and small girls named Hilary—"

"That's enough!" said Mr. Hummer. He turned to Hilary. "Your mother and I have been patient, but this owl business is interfering with your schoolwork."

"Starting tomorrow you're to walk straight to school," said Mrs. Hummer. "You're not to give anyone your homework. You're not to give anyone your watch—"

"I don't have a watch," said Hilary.

"You're not to give anyone anything."

Mr. Hummer nodded. "Otherwise we'll have no choice but to take turns walking you to school."

"*Walking* me?" Hilary sat up straight.

"You can't do that. Everyone will laugh at her," said Angelica.

Jack nodded. "Only kindergartners get walked to school."

Hilary was glad to have Angelica and Jack on her side, but that didn't change the terrible news.

Mr. Hummer gave her a serious look. "It's up to you, Hilary. Either you get your homework safely to school, starting tomorrow. Or one of us will go along with you."

Jack and Angelica shook their heads. "Poor Hilary."

That night as she did her homework, Hilary practiced saying, *"Out of my way, owl! Take a hike, owl! Owl, I'm not giving you homework!"*

"*Nffit-nffit-nffit,*" sniffed Clover encouragingly.

"I'll bet I know what the owl will do," said Hilary. "Peck me with its dangerous beak. Grab me in its powerful claws. Fly me high above town and let me drop." She went back to her owl homework. "I hope Mom and Dad will be happy then!"

"Breakfast, Hilary!"

The next morning Hilary felt too nervous to eat her French toast. She felt too nervous to listen to Angelica's and Jack's jokes. Instead, she gathered her books early and left for school.

As she hurried along the sidewalk, she practiced what she would say when the owl appeared. *"Get lost, owl! Take a hike, owl! Owl, I'm not giving you homework!* Oh, no!"

The giant owl stepped out of the bushes. "I'm hungry," said the owl. "Give me homework to eat."

All the brave words she'd practiced went out of Hilary's head. She clutched her notebook and stepped backward. Her heart thumped, *Brmm—brmm—brmm—*

"Give me homework. Or else!" The owl stepped so close, its damp breath fogged Hilary's

glasses. Its old-clothes odor filled her nose.

Hilary couldn't help herself. She opened her notebook. She took out her homework paper.

"Fractions?" said the owl.

Hilary shook her head.

"State capitals?"

She shook her head, again. "Because of you, the whole class had to do this special report, 'Facts About Owls.'"

The bird cocked its head. "Owls? My favorite subject is owls. Before I eat that homework, read one or two facts to me."

"I'll be late," said Hilary.

The owl glared.

Hilary cleared her throat and read, "'Owls have large heads, curved claws, and short beaks. They eat insects, rodents, and smaller birds—'"

"What about homework?" said the owl.

Hilary checked her report and shook her head. "Wristwatches?"

She shook her head again. "'They hunt at night. During the day, they sleep—'"

"What was that?" said the owl.

"'During the day, they sleep,'" repeated Hilary.

"Let me see that." The owl snatched the report out of Hilary's hand.

Hilary cried, "Look out! You're crumpling it. Your beak will tear it—"

The owl looked at the paper and blinked. "'Hunt at night . . . during the day . . . Sleep—' No wonder other owls aren't friendly with me!"

That night at dinner Mrs. Hummer said, "Jack, how did you do on your geography test?"

Jack reached for the grated cheese. "Dynamite! I was the first one finished. I got six questions wrong, but I finished before anyone else."

"I can see we'll have to do some drilling," said Mr. Hummer. He turned to Angelica. "How did this afternoon's soccer practice go?"

Angelica twirled a strand of spaghetti. "All right, except I got stuck playing goalie. Mary Lou Gallagher kicked a ball right into my stomach."

Mr. Hummer shook his head sympathetically.

The table was quiet while everyone ate.

"Isn't anyone going to ask me about my day?" said Hilary.

Mrs. Hummer looked at Mr. Hummer.

Mr. Hummer cleared his throat. "Very well, Hilary. How was your day?"

Hilary straightened her glasses. "Excellent. I was chosen Class Messenger. My bean plant grew another inch, and the giant owl—"

"We'll have no more talk about giant owls," said Mr. Hummer.

"Let her tell!" said Angelica.

Mrs. Hummer nodded. "I'm curious. Let's hear."

Mr. Hummer looked around the table and frowned. He sighed then and shrugged.

"What about that owl?" said Jack.

"Wel-ll—" Hilary sat up straighter. "The owl stopped me and said, 'Give me your homework,' but when I told him it was a report about owls, he said, 'Read it aloud first.' So I read, and when I got to the part that said, 'Owls hunt at night and sleep during the day,' he said, 'But it's daytime now.' So I said, 'That's right, owl.' And he flew away!"

For a moment everyone was silent.

"Giant homework-eating owls don't just give up and fly away," said Jack.

Hilary shrugged. "This one did."

Angelica twirled spaghetti and said, "Isn't it funny how that bird took off just as Mom and Dad were threatening to walk to school with Hilary?"

Mr. Hummer cleared his throat. "Now that Hilary's gotten rid of the—uh—bird, we won't have to walk with her."

Mrs. Hummer nodded. "However she managed it, Hilary kept her part of the bargain. She turned in her homework, and I'll bet she received a fine grade."

Hilary sighed. "Not *that* fine. Mr. Caruso said my information was good, but he only gave me a C-plus."

"C-plus? That doesn't seem fair," said Mr. Hummer.

Hilary picked up her fork and started to twirl a strand of spaghetti. "He took off for sloppiness. It wasn't my fault, but by the time I turned in my paper, it *was* a little crumpled and torn."

"Torn?" said Jack.

"Crumpled?" said Angelica.

Hilary paused with the spaghetti halfway to her mouth. "Besides that, Mr. Caruso said it smelled."

"Smelled?" said Mrs. Hummer.

Hilary looked at her forkful of spaghetti. "He was right. It did smell. Exactly like a pile of old clothes."

2 | Sheep Tricks

On Monday evening Mr. Hummer made Hilary's favorite chili for dinner. Hilary ate three bites and put down her fork. After dinner, Mrs. Hummer challenged her to a game of checkers. Hilary couldn't concentrate.

"You seem nervous," said Mr. Hummer.

"Are you worried about something at school?" said Mrs. Hummer.

"Hilary's worried about dancing class," said Angelica. She looked at Jack, and they both snickered. "Grade schoolers always worry about that."

"You just be quiet," cried Hilary. Angelica and Jack were always making fun of her. Besides, what they said about her and dancing class was true.

"Oh, dancing class!" chuckled Mr. Hummer. "Does that start this week?"

"It starts Thursday," said Hilary. "Boys have to ask girls to dance. Girls have to ask boys. What if the boy I ask says no?"

"She's talking about Dexter Small," said Angelica. "Hilary may be very young, but she has sort of a crush on him."

Hilary's face got hot. Whenever she thought about Dexter her face got hot. Whenever she saw him, a ticklish feeling filled her chest.

"Dexter is probably just as anxious to be asked as you are to ask him," said Mrs. Hummer.

Mr. Hummer patted Hilary's shoulder. "The trick to handling a worrisome problem is to face it right away. First thing tomorrow, walk straight up to Dexter and ask him."

"Wel-ll—" Hilary wasn't sure. Lots of things she said and did at school made people laugh. Even her friends laughed. Dexter included. If she asked him to dance—

"What's the worst that could happen?" said Mrs. Hummer.

Angelica laughed so hard she started to choke. "Dexter could say, 'Dance with you, Hilary Hummer? I'd rather eat worms!'"

"That will be all, Angelica," said Mr. Hummer.

Hilary wailed, "She's right. He could!"

The next morning Hilary remembered her father's advice. As soon as she got to school, she looked for Dexter.

He wasn't at his desk. He wasn't at the coat closet or the pencil sharpener. Then she spotted

him in the classroom's garden corner. He was watering the potted ferns.

Hilary's face got hot. The ticklish feeling filled her chest.

I could ask him now, she thought. But her throat felt tight. Her legs wouldn't move.

"Hey, Hilary, want to help feed the turtles?" said Emily.

"Turtles?" said Hilary. "Yes." She hurried out of the classroom and down the hall to get fresh water. While the rest room faucet ran and the water dish filled, she thought, I'll ask Dexter later this morning. I will. I will.

But when the final bell rang that afternoon, Hilary still hadn't done it.

That night Hilary lost all her hotels and money playing Monopoly. She ended the game in jail.

"You really must be upset," said Mr. Hummer. "You're usually the big winner in these games."

Hilary lifted her marker from the board. "I'm so upset, I didn't sleep at all last night."

"When I have trouble sleeping, I count sheep,"

said Mr. Hummer. "Soft, gentle, comforting sheep. They really soothe a person's nerves."

"I count sheep, too," said Mrs. Hummer. "Fuzzy, calm, cuddly sheep. And little lambs . . ."

Jack said, "When I can't sleep, I count all the times that nice girls like Hilary asked me to dance, and I said, 'N—O—NO!'"

"Don't be such a tease, Jack," said Mr. Hummer.

Mrs. Hummer said, "Never mind, Hilary. You count those sheep, and I guarantee you'll get a good night's rest."

"I'd get a better night's rest if I could just skip dancing class," said Hilary.

"None of that," said Mr. Hummer.

"Off to bed," said Mrs. Hummer.

Hilary trudged to her room. She said goodnight to Clover, climbed into bed, and slipped into uneasy sleep.

Tick—tock—tick—
The next thing she knew, Hilary was wide

awake. Moonlight streamed through her window. Outside, the street was empty. Inside, the house was dark and quiet. Only the hall clock sounded, *Tick–tock–tick—*

Dancing class! thought Hilary. Dexter! thought Hilary. What if I ask him and he says no? Her cheeks got hot. Her hands started to sweat. She was about to get up for a glass of water when she remembered her parents' advice. Soft sheep. Fluffy sheep. Soothing sheep.

I'll count some, thought Hilary. She lay back on her pillow to concentrate.

Tick–tock–tick—

A soft green pasture unrolled before her. Across the pasture, a low fence unwound. Beside the fence, sunlight sparkled on a little pond. Beside the pond a flock of woolly sheep baaahed and grazed under the clear blue sky.

Hilary yawned and waited.

A fluffy sheep ran for the fence. It jumped, sailed smoothly over, and landed softly on the other side.

"One," counted Hilary. She felt calmer already. Asking Dexter wouldn't be so scary. Why shouldn't he say yes?

A second sheep ran for the fence. It jumped, sailed smoothly over, and landed softly on the other side.

"Two," yawned Hilary. Her eyelids felt heavy. She yawned some more.

A third sheep ran for the fence.

Hilary thought, Tomorrow I'll walk straight up to Dexter. I'll say, Dexter—

The sheep reached the fence, but instead of jumping, it dug in its heels and skidded to a stop.

That sheep was supposed to jump, thought Hilary.

The sheep shook itself and trotted away from the fence to munch grass.

"Jump," said Hilary.

The sheep paid no attention.

Hilary turned to another sheep. "Will *you* jump?"

"Baa-ah-ah-aah!" That sheep turned its back and cantered away.

"Somebody's got to jump!" Hilary looked from one sheep to another.

Every one of those sheep lay down on the grass.

"Please?" said Hilary.

"Baa-ah-ah-aah!" The sheep looked back at her and wouldn't budge.

The next morning at breakfast Mrs. Hummer said, "You don't look well, Hilary. Are you coming down with a cold?"

"Hilary's coming down with cold feet," said Angelica. "Only two more days and she still hasn't asked Dexter if he'll dance with her."

"You're still worrying about dancing class?" said Mr. Hummer.

"I woke up in the middle of the night, and I couldn't go back to sleep," said Hilary. "I think I'd better skip dancing class until I feel better."

"Nonsense," said Mrs. Hummer.

Mr. Hummer patted Hilary's shoulder. "You forgot the secret weapon. You forgot to count sheep."

"I didn't forget," said Hilary. "Those pesky sheep wouldn't behave. They ate grass, baaahed, and wouldn't jump the fence. No matter what I said!"

"I've never heard of such a thing," said Mrs. Hummer.

Mr. Hummer frowned. "Counting sheep are usually so well behaved. Perhaps you weren't firm enough when you asked."

"Wel-ll—" said Hilary. "I thought I was."

Jack nudged Angelica. "Hilary had better be a lot more firm when she asks Dexter."

Angelica said, "*When?* The way Hilary's dragging her heels, I'd make that *if.*"

They both laughed so hard, Mr. Hummer made them leave the table.

That day at school Mr. Caruso called on Hilary during arithmetic class. Hilary was so sleepy she didn't hear.

"I'm speaking to you, Hilary," said Mr. Caruso. "Is the answer to this problem four gallons or twelve gallons?"

"Twelve sheep," said Hilary.

Everyone snickered.

From his seat two rows ahead, Dexter turned to look at her. "Twelve *sheep*?"

Hilary's face got hot. The ticklish feeling filled

her chest. Those sheep are ruining everything! she thought. While the arithmetic lesson went on, she scribbled a picture of a fluffy, obedient sheep in her workbook. But when she put down her pencil and sat back to look, even that sheep looked smart-alecky. Even that sheep looked as though it would ignore whatever she said.

That evening at bedtime, Hilary's mother read her a funny story.

"That will help you sleep," said Mrs. Hummer.

Mr. Hummer brought her a cup of warm milk. "Don't think about dancing class or Dexter or any other worrisome thing."

"I'll try not to," said Hilary. She drank the milk, closed her eyes, and fell asleep.

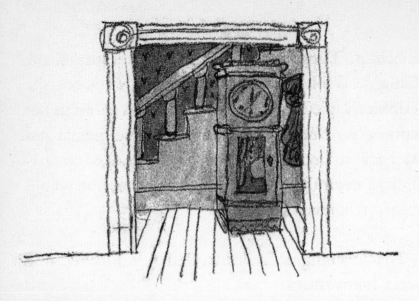

Tick–tock–tick—

The next thing she knew, Hilary was wide awake. Moonlight streamed through her window. Outside, the street was empty. Inside, the house was dark and quiet. Only the hall clock sounded, *Tick–tock–tick—*

Dancing class! thought Hilary. Dexter! thought Hilary. Before she could stop herself she thought, Sheep!

A soft green pasture unrolled before her. Across the pasture, a low fence unwound. Beside the fence, sunlight sparkled on a little pond. Beside the pond, the same flock of woolly sheep baaahed and grazed.

Hilary remembered what Mr. Hummer had said about being firm. She made her voice deep and steady. "Line up, you sheep!"

The sheep kept munching grass.

"Line up!" said Hilary.

The sheep baaahed, moved to another spot, and munched some more.

"Jump that fence!" said Hilary. "That's an order."

The sheep looked at the fence. They looked at Hilary. *"Baa-ah-ah-aah!"* They rolled on their backs in the soft green grass and ignored her.

The next morning Hilary was yawning so hard she could barely swallow her pancakes.

"Did those sheep misbehave again last night?" said Mr. Hummer.

Hilary said, "They behaved worse than ever. I said, 'Line up! Jump that fence!' I used my firmest voice, and they paid no attention to me."

"I can't understand it," said Mr. Hummer. He got up to clear the table.

Mrs. Hummer got up to clear, too. "Sheep can be sensitive. Perhaps you frightened them."

"Frightened them?" Hilary thought about how the sheep had stared at her, how they baaahed and rolled in the grass. "Those sheep didn't act frightened. They acted like sheep who enjoyed making me upset."

Jack leaned toward Hilary and grinned. "Speaking of upset, tomorrow afternoon is dancing class. Time's running out for you to ask Dexter."

Hilary stared at her cold pancakes. "Today I'll do it. Don't think I won't. I've made up my mind. Today I'll ask him!"

That morning at recess Hilary stood on the playground and argued with herself. I'm going to ask him! Maybe I shouldn't. I'll ask right now! Maybe I'll wait till after lunch—

"Come play kickball!" shouted Dean and Lesley.

"Not now," said Hilary.

Erin and Randall shouted, "Come run races!"

"Maybe later," said Hilary. She edged over to the diamond where Jared, Dexter, and Donna were playing Whiffle ball. Donna was pitching, Jared was catching, and Dexter was at bat. Hilary's face felt hot. The ticklish feeling filled her chest.

Donna got ready to pitch.

Dexter pulled back the bat to swing.

Wouldn't everyone be surprised if I walked up to Dexter right now, thought Hilary. Wouldn't

they be surprised if Dexter smiled and said, "I was hoping you'd ask." Tonight those troublemaking sheep wouldn't have anything to say but—

"Hey, Hilary," yelled Jared. "Want to play?"

"Baa-ah-aah—" The sound came out before Hilary could stop it.

Dexter swung, but he was laughing so hard he missed.

"Strike!" yelled Donna.

"That pitch doesn't count," said Dexter. He pointed the bat to where Hilary stood with her hands clapped over her mouth. "There was unfair interference from sheep!"

That night Mr. and Mrs. Hummer made a big thing of not mentioning dancing class. They made a big thing of not mentioning sheep. They hushed Angelica and Jack when they tried to bring up either one.

Angelica and Jack weren't ready to give up. After Hilary went to bed, they crouched outside her room and made noises through the door.

"*Ba-ah-ah-ah-aah,* I'm a soft, fluffy sheep and even *I* won't listen to Hilary."

"Quiet! I'm trying to sleep," yelled Hilary.

They kept it up. "I'm popular Dexter Small. If a sheep won't listen to Hilary, why should I?"

Hilary clapped her hands over her ears. "My ears are covered. I can't hear you. You're wasting your breath!"

"I'm a fluffy sheep. *Bah-ah-ah-aah*—"

"I can't hear you. I can't hear you. I can't hear you!" Hilary kept it up until she fell asleep.

Tick–tock–tick—

The next thing she knew, Hilary was wide awake. Moonlight streamed through her window. Outside, the street was empty. Inside, the house was dark and quiet. Only the hall clock sounded, *Tick–tock–tick—*

Dancing class! thought Hilary. Dexter! thought Hilary. Before she could stop herself, she thought, Oh no, sheep!

The soft green pasture unrolled before her. Across the pasture unwound the low gray fence. Beside the fence, sunlight sparkled off a little pond. Beside the pond—

The grass was empty.

Empty? thought Hilary. She looked from one

end of the pasture to the other. Empty? She couldn't see even one soft, fluffy sheep.

Where did they go? she wondered. If those sheep aren't in their pasture, where are they?

Tick–tock–tick— sounded the old hall clock. *Tock–tick–tock—*

Those no-good sheep! They're up to something, thought Hilary. Her eyelids grew heavy. They drooped. They closed. Tomorrow . . . thought Hilary. Dexter . . . thought Hilary. She fell asleep wondering, Where *are* those troublemaking sheep?

The next morning as Hilary left the house, Angelica yelled, "Have fun at dancing class!"

Hilary slammed the front door and trudged off to school. The skirt of her pink-and-white party dress bounced as she crossed Beech Street. The toes of her dress-up shoes tip-tapped as she climbed the school's front steps. As she opened the classroom door, her pink-and-white hair ribbon fluttered.

"Don't you look nice," said Mr. Caruso.

"Thank you," said Hilary, but her stomach felt nervous as she hung her sweater in the coat closet. Her hands felt sweaty as she took her seat by the window.

Dexter sat at his desk in the row ahead. His hair was neatly combed. His shoes were brightly polished. When Hilary looked at him in his suit and tie, her chest filled with the familiar ticklish feeling. He was rearranging papers in his notebook. She thought, I could ask him now. I could say— *"Baa-ah-ah-ahh—"*

Hilary froze. Slowly, reluctantly, she turned to look out the window.

The whole flock of troublemaking sheep was milling around on the grass. "Scat! Get out of here," she hissed.

"Did you say something to me?"

Hilary spun around. Instantly, her face got hot. The ticklish feeling filled her chest. Dexter had turned and was looking straight at her. "It sounded like you. It sounded like one of your loud whispers."

Hilary shook her head hard. "It wasn't."

Dexter shrugged and went back to tidying his notebook.

Hilary glanced out the window and hissed, "Go away."

The sheep moved closer.

She made shooing motions. "Get back!"

Three small sheep climbed on the others' backs, pressed their noses to the window, and nudged one another when they caught sight of Dexter. Their sides shook as though they were laughing.

Hilary shook her fist. "Get baa—"

"You *did* say something to me!"

She turned from the window. Dexter was staring right at her.

"What did you say? Or were you just imitating sheep?"

For a minute, Hilary couldn't speak. She couldn't swallow or even breathe. She looked at Dexter and then she heard herself whisper, "If I asked you to dance this afternoon, what would you say?"

Tick–tock—, ticked the classroom clock.

"Dance with you?" said Dexter.

Hilary nodded.

Outside the window, the sheep leaned closer.

"You're always doing crazy things," said Dexter.

Hilary fiddled with a pencil and wished she could disappear.

"You make me laugh a lot." Dexter shrugged. "I'd say, okay."

"Okay?" said Hilary.

Dexter nodded.

Hilary turned to the sheep outside the window and hissed, "I guess I showed you. I guess I showed Angelica. And Jack, too!"

"Baa-ah-ah-ahh—" The three small sheep slid grumpily down off the others. As they joined the flock milling below the window, they gave her dirty looks. *"Baa-ah-ah-ahh—"*

Hilary pointed past them to where the fence ran around the playing field. "I've had just about enough of your bad behavior. Go!"

"Baa-ah-ah-ahh—" The sheep slunk across the field to the fence.

"Jump!" said Hilary.

One sheep ran for the fence, jumped, and sailed over it. Another followed. A third jumped, and a fourth—

As they went, Hilary counted, "Five, six, seven—"

"Hilary!"

Hilary blinked.

Everyone, including Dexter, was staring at her.

Mr. Caruso stood at the blackboard. "I've been speaking to you, Hilary. Is the answer to this problem five more yards or five more feet?"

Hilary straightened her glasses. "That's easy. The answer to this problem is *no more sheep!*"

"Sheep?" Everyone snickered, Dexter included.

Hilary didn't care. She knew she was right.

3

Snow People

When Uncle Gary and Aunt Deb had to go out of town on a December business trip, they left their little boy, Geoff, with Hilary's family. They left their cat, Growl, as well.

"*Pdrrrrrrrrrrr—*" Growl rubbed against Hilary's leg and made figure eights around her ankles.

"Growl tickles!" said Hilary.

Uncle Gary handed Mr. Hummer a large brown bag. "Here's a supply of Growl's food. He eats one can every day."

Aunt Deb said, "Here are Geoff's jars of baby

food. Here's his favorite stuffed toy, and here's his special blanket."

"Geoff mustn't be overexcited, overtired, overheated, or overchilled," said Uncle Gary. "And each afternoon, he needs a long nap."

Angelica looked at the baby in his playpen. "Poor Geoff."

Jack said, "Doesn't he ever have fun?"

"Il-*ree!*" Geoff reached out and grabbed Hilary's hand.

Hilary looked down at him and smiled. It was going to be nice having someone in the house who was younger than she was. Someone who would look up to her. Someone she could teach things to. "I'll make sure you have fun. I'll take good care of you, too."

Angelica was rehearsing with the junior high drama club the next afternoon. Jack was playing in a junior high hockey game. Mr. Hummer was in the kitchen writing a grocery list while Mrs. Hummer got Geoff ready for his nap. Hilary sat on the window seat and watched snow fall past the living room window. Growl sat beside her and watched, too. The flakes were big and damp. Perfect for building snowmen.

"We'd better hurry," Mr. Hummer called from

the hallway. He was wearing his parka and carrying the shopping list. He turned to Hilary. "We're counting on you to be a good baby-sitter. Are you sure you can manage?"

"I'm as big as Angelica and Jack were when they started baby-sitting for me. I'm going to be the best baby-sitter Geoff ever had." Hilary climbed off the window seat and followed Mr. Hummer to Geoff's room.

"Il-*ree!*" said Geoff.

Mrs. Hummer covered Geoff with his special blanket and tiptoed from the room. "If Geoff wakes before we get home, Hilary, you may pick him up and give him some juice. While he rests,

you may read, watch TV, or play music very quietly."

Hilary watched as Mrs. Hummer pulled on her parka and stepped into her boots. "I won't have time for reading or TV. While you're at the store, I'm going outside to build a snowman."

Mrs. Hummer kissed her good-bye. "Not today. Today, it's your job to stay inside and look after Geoff."

"Inside?" said Hilary. "Can't I baby-sit from the front yard?"

Mrs. Hummer shook her head. "You can build your snowman some other day."

"Geoff's counting on you," said Mr. Hummer. "We are, too."

Hilary sat on the window seat and watched the snow fall. The fattest, fluffiest flakes she had ever seen blanketed the lawn and coated the driveway.

"Pdrrrrrrrrrrrrr—" Growl sat and watched, too.

"Tomorrow, that snow will be no good for packing," said Hilary. "Tomorrow, it might even

melt. The time to build a snowman is right now, today."

"Pdrrrrrrrrrrrrrr—" Growl watched a mound of snow slip off the oak tree and crash silently onto the snowy lawn.

"I'll bet Geoff has never built a snowman," said Hilary. "If we went outside and brought him with us, I could teach him how."

Growl watched a chickadee hop out of the Hummer's hedge and onto their whitened driveway.

Hilary said, "You know Geoff better than I do. Would he rather stay inside and nap, or go out?"

As the bird hopped closer, Growl's ears stiffened. His back rose. He sprang at the glass. *"Rrrgwwww!"*

Hilary jumped off the window seat. "All right! Let's go."

Growl followed Hilary as she helped Geoff, dressed in his boots and snowsuit, totter down the front steps and across the snow-covered lawn. At the center of the lawn Hilary stopped. "If we build the snowman here, Mom and Dad will see it as soon as they get home. They'll know we went outside, and I'll be in big trouble."

"Tuh-buh!" said Geoff.

Growl hunted under the hedge for the chickadee. *"Maooow."*

Hilary looked to one side of the house. She looked to the other. She looked down the driveway to the

empty field on the other side of Partridge Lane. "That's the place for a snowman!"

"Tha-sa-pways!" said Geoff.

"Pdrrrrrrrrr—" Growl came out from under the hedge to agree.

Hilary rolled one giant snowball. She rolled two giant snowballs. She rolled three giant snowballs.

She built the biggest snowman Growl or Geoff had ever seen.

"No-man!" said Geoff.

"He looks lonely," said Hilary. She rolled three

more large snowballs, and beside the snowman, she built an extra-large snow woman. She stepped back to look at the huge snow couple. "Wow!"

Growl made figure eights around the bases of the snow people. *"Pdrrrrrrrrrr—"*

"What this snowman and snow woman need is a snow family." Hilary rolled three medium-size snowballs and built a medium-size snow boy. "Now I'll build a snow girl—"

"Cohd," said Geoff.

"Maooooow," whined Growl.

Hilary straightened up. Her arms ached and she was panting. "You're right, Geoff. It is cold. I

think you've learned enough stuff for one afternoon. Besides, Mom and Dad will be home any
minute. We'd better get inside before they see us."

Snow was still falling when Mr. and Mrs. Hummer got home from the store. Mr. Hummer pulled
off his gloves and stamped snow off his boots.
"We were gone a long time. Did you have any
trouble? Did Geoff fuss?"

"Not a bit," said Hilary.

"Did you see what someone built in the empty

field?" Mrs. Hummer unzipped her parka. "Three handsome snow people."

"Snow people?" said Hilary.

"Hilary was too busy baby-sitting to notice," said Mr. Hummer. He reached into one of the grocery bags, pulled out a big green-and-yellow box, and handed it to Hilary. "You gave up an outdoor afternoon to look after Geoff. You deserve a reward."

"New crayons!" Hilary opened the box. Rose

red. Cobalt blue. Maize. Chartreuse. There were sixty-four different colors. Each had a sharp, perfect point. Each had a tidy paper wrapping. "My old box doesn't have half as many colors. Most are broken. None have points, and all the wrappers are ripped off."

Mrs. Hummer smiled as she hung up her parka. "You earned them by being a grown-up, trust-worthy baby-sitter."

"Oh, that," said Hilary. She thought of the snow people standing in a row in the dark field across the street. She thought of all the time she'd kept Geoff outdoors when he was supposed to be napping. She looked at her new crayons and didn't feel excited anymore.

"*Maow*—" mewed Growl from under the kitchen table.

Growl knows I wasn't a good baby-sitter, thought Hilary. She looked at Geoff. He yawned and rubbed his eyes. She looked at her mother and father and wondered, Will they find out?

"*Maow*—" Growl made figure eights around Hilary's ankles.

Hilary straightened her glasses and thought, Growl won't tell on me. She felt a little better. If Growl didn't tell, who else could?

Tpp—tpp—tpp—
That night a strange noise woke Hilary.
Tpp—tpp—tpp—
Someone was tapping on her bedroom window. Could it be Growl? wondered Hilary. Then she thought, Growl wouldn't be outside. Growl's asleep in the kitchen.
Tpp—tpp—tpp—
Hilary climbed out of bed. *Sswwwsh,* she pulled back the curtain.

A large white face peered in at her.

It was the snow boy.

Hilary opened the window. "What do you want?"

The snow boy held out his snow hand. "I want your new crayons. The ones with the sharp points and the sixty-four colors. Hand them over or I'll tell your parents how you disobeyed."

Hilary felt cold all over. She opened her mouth, but no sound came out.

"Let's have those crayons!" said the snow boy.

Hilary handed him the large green–and–yellow box.

The next morning Hilary walked down the driveway on her way to school. The snow people stood in the field across the street and watched.

"Go away!" said Hilary.

The snow people stayed where they were. They put their heads together and whispered. All the while they kept their eyes on her.

At school Hilary tried not to think about the snow people. She did ten arithmetic problems. She painted a picture of a moose and wrote down five facts about moose and their habits. After lunch Mr. Caruso explained the correct way to write a business letter. Hilary copied the example.

"Very good," said Mr. Caruso. "But remember, drop the 'e' from 'true' when you write 'truly.'"

Hilary nodded. During reading hour, she read a story about a magic fish who granted wishes.

I wish . . . thought Hilary. She had an idea and wrote a business letter of her own.

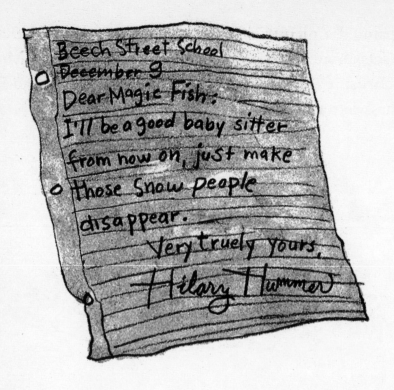

Beech Street School
December 9
Dear Magic Fish:
I'll be a good baby sitter
from now on, just make
those snow people
disappear.
Very truely yours,
Hilary Hummer

Hilary folded the letter and slipped it into her desk.

As she walked home from school that afternoon, Hilary crossed her fingers and hoped. She kept hoping until she reached the corner where Beech Street met Partridge Lane. Please, she thought as she paused on the sidewalk. When I turn the corner, let those snow people be gone!

She eased around the corner and peered down the street, into the field.

The snow people peered back.

While Hilary did homework in her room, the snow people watched from the field across the street. While Hilary and her family sat at the dinner table, they watched, too. While Angelica went to the kitchen to get dessert, Mrs. Hummer checked

Hilary's homework. Mr. Hummer and Jack talked about Jack's new hockey skates. "This is a fine business letter Hilary has written as homework," said Mrs. Hummer, handing Mr. Hummer the letter.

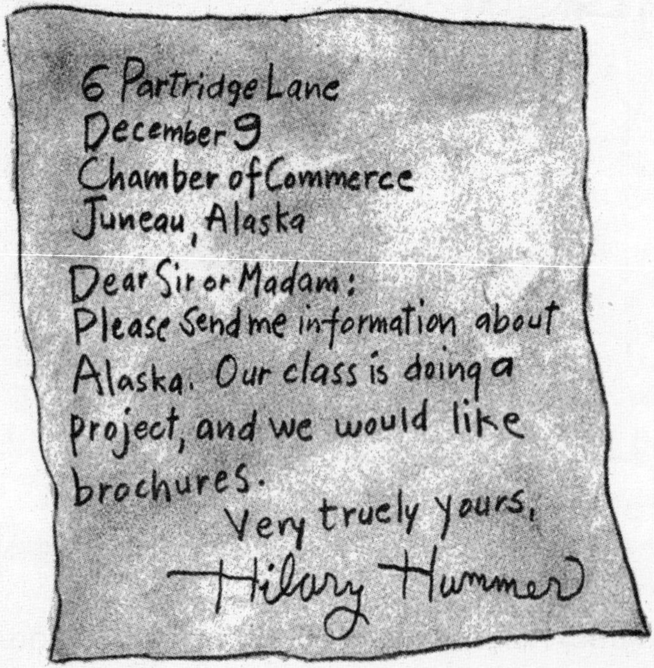

6 Partridge Lane
December 9
Chamber of Commerce
Juneau, Alaska

Dear Sir or Madam:
Please send me information about Alaska. Our class is doing a project, and we would like brochures.
Very truely yours,
Hilary Hummer

"Very good," Mr. Hummer handed the letter back to Hilary. "But remember. When you write 'truly,' drop the 'e.'"

"Eeeeeeee!" Geoff pounded his high chair tray.

Jack said, "I wish we lived in Alaska. I could use my hockey skates all year long."

"I'll bet those snow people in the field wish that they lived in Alaska," said Mr. Hummer. "They'd never melt."

I'd like to send them to Alaska, thought Hilary. Or someplace where it's very, very warm!

"Who's ready for angel food cake?" Angelica stepped through the door from the kitchen.

"Angel food cake!" said Jack. It was the whole family's favorite dessert.

Angelica cut the pieces and handed them around.

Jack made sure everyone's slice was exactly the same size.

Hilary picked up her fork and took a bite. She chewed, but she couldn't enjoy the cake. She might as well have been eating cardboard. Three pairs of eyes followed her every move. Three voices muttered about her in the dark.

Nasty snow people, I never should have built you! thought Hilary.

Tpp—tpp—tpp—

"Go away!" said Hilary that night when the tapping began.

Tpp—tpp—tpp—

In a minute the noise will wake Mom and Dad, thought Hilary. She crept to the window, pulled back a corner of the curtain, and peered out.

A large white face peered in at her.

Tpp—tpp—tpp—

It was the snow woman.

Hilary opened the window.

"I want cake." The snow woman closed a large cold hand around Hilary's wrist. "Bring me a piece of that delicious-looking angel food cake you had for dinner!"

"I'm not allowed to take angel food cake in the middle of the night." Hilary tried to pull her wrist free.

The snow woman tightened her grip. "Bring me cake, or I'll tell your parents what you did while they were at the grocery store!"

Hilary yanked her arm away. She pulled on her bathrobe and opened the bedroom door.

The snow woman called after her. "Bring cake for snowman and snow boy, too. Be sure to cut large pieces!"

Hilary hurried down the dark hallway, through the dining room, into the kitchen. The house was warm, but she felt cold all over. She looked at Growl dozing on his cushion beside the kitchen table. "Why did you make me build those snow people?"

Growl sat up and blinked. *"Maow?"*

Hilary cut one slice of angel food cake. Two

slices. Three. She slapped them onto a large paper plate and hurried back to her room.

"Here's your cake," she said to the snow woman. "Now leave me alone!" She slammed the window and went back to bed.

The next morning at breakfast Angelica said, "Someone was talking to herself in the kitchen late last night. It sounded a lot like Hilary."

"Il-*ree!*" Geoff pounded his high chair tray.

Everyone else looked at Hilary and waited.

Hilary straightened her glasses. "I wasn't talking to myself. I was talking to Growl. He wanted water, and I got it for him."

Jack pointed to the cake plate on the kitchen counter. "You wanted seconds on dessert. Half the angel food cake is gone, and there's a trail of cake crumbs leading right to your door!"

"Il-*ree*!" Geoff stamped on his high chair footrest.

Mrs. Hummer cleared her throat. "We all like angel food cake. It wasn't fair of you to take the lion's share."

Hilary stared at her poached egg and wished that those sneaked slices *had* been a share for a lion.

Mr. Hummer frowned. "You know better than to take snacks from the kitchen at night. Still, it's hard to be angry with you after you've taken such good care of Geoff."

Hilary looked at Growl.

Growl looked at Hilary.

Mrs. Hummer said, "Let's settle things this way. When we finish up the cake for dessert tonight, Hilary will skip it and have fruit instead. Does that sound fair to everyone?"

Jack looked at Angelica.

Angelica chewed her lip and frowned for a minute, then she nodded.

"Sounds fair to me," said Mr. Hummer.

Jack said, "All right, but remember, just fruit.

Hilary doesn't get even one crumb of cake!"

Everyone nodded.

Greedy, troublemaking snow people! thought Hilary.

That night the tapping began as usual.

Tpp—tpp—tpp—

"The angel food cake's all gone," cried Hilary. Her toes and fingers felt cold. Her stomach felt jumpy. She wished the night would be over and it would get light.

Tpp—tpp—tpp—

"Clover, what can they want now?" she whispered.

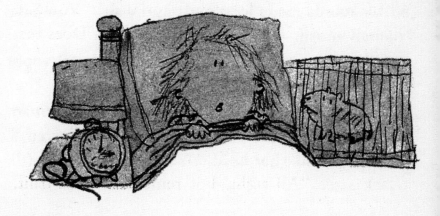

Tpp—tpp—tpp—

Hilary climbed out of bed and tiptoed to Clover's cage. She slid open the door and reached inside. "You come with me and look fierce." She cradled Clover in one hand. With the other, she swept back the curtain. *Sswwwh—*

The snowman stared in at her. "Open this window!"

Hilary opened it.

"Snow woman and I want a playmate for snow boy."

Hilary shivered. "I was going to build you a snow girl, but I ran out of time."

"A snow girl is not what we want." The snowman's words made ice clouds in the air. "You have a small cousin. We want him!"

Hilary opened her mouth, but only a vapor cloud came out.

"Give us your small cousin," said the snowman. "Or we'll tell your parents how you disobeyed."

Hilary shook her head. "You can't have Geoff!"

The snowman stretched a cold hand toward Clover. "In that case, I'll take your beast."

"No!" Hilary snatched away Clover and ran.

"Mom!" She burst into her parents' bedroom. "Dad! Mom! Don't let them take Clover! Don't let them take Geoff!"

"Hilary?" Mrs. Hummer sat up in bed.

Mr. Hummer sat up beside her. "What on earth is happening?"

"The snow people are after me!" said Hilary. "The snow people from across the street."

"What's going on?" Jack stumbled in, rubbing his eyes.

Angelica followed him. "A person can't get any sleep!"

"Those snow people come to my window every night. First they took my crayons. Then they took all that angel food cake. Tonight they wanted to take Geoff! When I said no, they tried to take Clover instead."

"*Chuukaa-chuukaa-chuukaa!*" chattered Clover.

Mr. Hummer frowned. "Why are these snow people after you? What did you do to them?"

"Nothing!" said Hilary. "I worked hard one whole afternoon to build them. Now this is the way they pay me back."

Mr. Hummer sat up straighter. "*You* built them?"

Mrs. Hummer switched on a light. "*Which* afternoon?"

"Wel-ll—" Hilary chewed her lip. She scratched her head. "I think it *may* have been that very same afternoon when I baby-sat so well for Geoff. . . ."

"Getting Geoff up from his nap and taking him outside was wrong." Mr. Hummer tucked Hilary back into bed. "Are you sorry you disobeyed?"

"I'm sorry," said Hilary.

"Are you sorry you misled us?" Mrs. Hummer

took Clover from Hilary and put her back in her cage.

"I'm sorry for that, too."

"Are you sorry you built those snow people?"

Hilary said, "Mom, Dad, I'm sorrier about that than about anything."

"All right," said Mr. Hummer. "Close your eyes and get some sleep."

"What if those snow people come back to my window?" whispered Hilary.

"I think you've seen the last of those snow people," said Mr. Hummer.

Angelica yawned. "It's not unusual for a guilty conscience to give a little child like you bad dreams."

"I'm not little, and it wasn't a dream," said Hilary.

Jack wagged a finger at her. "A bad dream could also come from eating several stolen pieces of angel food cake."

"That's enough, Jack!" Mr. Hummer shooed everyone from the room and pulled Hilary's door shut behind them.

Hilary turned to Clover. "No one believes me!"

"*Nnnffffffff* . . ." Clover was already fast asleep.

The next morning Hilary was late coming to the kitchen for breakfast.

When she finally appeared, Mrs. Hummer said, "I'm not surprised you overslept. That bad dream gave you quite a scare."

Mr. Hummer nodded. "It kept you awake for a long time, too."

"Il-*ree!*" Geoff waved his cereal spoon in the air.

Hilary slammed a used paper plate and a battered box of crayons onto the breakfast table. "It wasn't

a dream. I can prove it. Those snow people came back to my window later last night, and look what they left!"

"Crayons?" said Angelica.

"My new box of crayons. The snow people broke lots and took the paper off most, but at least I got back what's left of them."

Jack pointed to the paper plate. "What's that?"

Hilary straightened her glasses. "The angel food cake plate. You can still see some crumbs. And look, on the back, the snow people wrote a confession."

"Confession?" said Mr. Hummer.

Hilary turned over the plate and pointed to rose red and cobalt blue lettering.

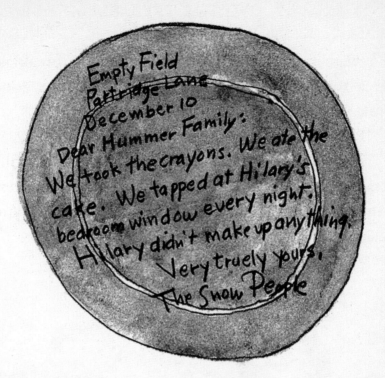

Empty Field
Partridge Lane
December 10
Dear Hummer Family:
We took the crayons. We ate the
cake. We tapped at Hilary's
bedroom window every night.
Hilary didn't make up anything.
Very truely yours,
The Snow People

Mrs. Hummer turned to Hilary. "The snow people wrote this?"

Hilary nodded. "Their consciences bothered them. Besides, I said I'd push them over if they didn't tell the truth. I guess now everyone has to believe me."

"*Maow*—" Growl padded under the breakfast table to lick up fallen cake crumbs.

"Let's see that confession." Angelica snatched

the plate from Hilary. She set it on the breakfast table where both she and Jack could take a good look.

"Hey—"

Hilary saw where Jack was pointing. She straightened her glasses quickly and said, "Careless snow people! Everyone knows that when you write 'truly,' you drop the 'e.'"

4 | Big Pig

For as long as she could remember, Hilary had loved going to the Penny Wise Savings Bank. It wasn't so that she could stare past the metal-barred grate into the vault. It wasn't because Ms. Primly, the manager, always gave her a lollipop. It was because atop the bank's flat roof, silhouetted against the sky, stood a pig the size of a mini-van.

PENNY WISE said the blue banner draped over the pig's right shoulder and across her chest. A penny as big as a manhole cover had frozen midway through the coin slot in her back. The pig's pink skin was smooth except inside her pointed ears, where it looked fuzzy. Her short tail curled. Her plump cheeks and squarish snout framed a kindly, understanding smile.

In stormy weather and in fair, Penny Wise watched over Old Shoreville and the people passing below on Beech Street. In daylight and in twilight, she kept her vigil on the bank's roof. Every person in town knew and loved Penny Wise, and Penny Wise knew and looked out for each of them.

When Hilary was just a baby in a car seat, driving with her parents past the bank, Penny Wise

watched. That reassuring pig watched Hilary's second-grade class visit the bank on a field trip. She watched Hilary bicycle by at age eight, jump rope by at nine, roller skate by at ten. Whenever Hilary passed the bank, whenever she climbed its steps, she could glance up and be sure of seeing Penny Wise smiling down upon her.

One January evening Hilary was in her room playing Forgotten Planet when she heard her parents arrive home from work.

"Hilary," called Mr. Hummer from the front hall. "Come see what we've brought you."

Hilary left her toys on their distant planet and ran to the hall. Jack appeared from the basement; Angelica, from the living room. Hilary took one look at what her mother was holding and could hardly speak. "Mine?"

"Ms. Primly was giving them away at the bank today." Mr. Hummer smiled as he hung his overcoat in the hall closet. "She thought you'd like one better than a lollipop."

It was much smaller than the rooftop pig, and it didn't have a giant penny stuck in its coin slot. But this lunch-box-size pink pig did have the same blue banner, fuzzy ears, and curly tail as the familiar giant on the bank roof. Hilary took the piggy bank from her mother and cradled it in her arms. "My own personal Penny Wise!"

Mr. Hummer pulled a quarter out of his trousers pocket. "Here's a little something to start your savings."

Clnnk! Hilary dropped it down the coin slot in the pig's back. Angelica and Jack each had a bank. Owning one made Hilary feel much more grown-up herself.

"And here's your allowance," Mrs. Hummer said, handing Hilary one dollar bill and three more quarters.

Angelica and Jack did whatever they wanted with their savings. When someone in the family had a birthday, Angelica and Jack each took money from their banks and bought an exciting present. Hilary thought, Now I'll be able to buy presents, too.

Clnnk-clnnk-clnnk!

Jack frowned and gave the pig a closer look. "There's something funny about this plastic pork chop."

"Don't call her that," said Hilary.

Angelica traced the pig's mouth with her finger.

"I'll tell you what it is. Penny Wise's smile is kind and understanding. This pig's smile is sort of sneaky."

"Sneaky?" Hilary turned the pig her way and looked.

"See?" said Angelica.

Hilary slowly nodded. There *was* something different about the smile—

"Nonsense!" Mrs. Hummer hung up her coat. "The smile is painted on a little crookedly. That's all."

Mr. Hummer agreed. "All this piglet needs to make it kind and understanding is a good home, lots of love, and lots of savings."

Hilary gave the little pig all three. She made a

place for the bank on the top bookshelf in her bed-room, and she took the little pig down at least once a day to stroke its ears and drop coins through its slot. Hilary saved pennies. She saved dimes. She saved her allowance and her leaf-raking money. The pig got heavier and heavier. Its smile got wider and wider, but it stayed crooked.

"I still say it's sneaky." Angelica barged into Hilary's room, plopped down on her bed, and stared at the pig on the top bookshelf.

Hilary didn't agree that it was sneaky. But it was the day before Jack's birthday, and she was too excited to argue. "I'm just about to take out my money. Tomorrow I'm going to buy Jack an aquarium!"

"An aquarium?" Angelica sat up straight.

Hilary nodded. "When Mom goes to the bakery

to pick up his birthday cake, she's going to take me to the pet shop to get it."

Angelica looked doubtful. "An aquarium—even a small one—costs a lot of money."

"I'll bet I have enough. I've been saving for weeks. Want to help me count?"

Angelica shook her head. "Too much home-work. Besides, I have soccer practice, and I still have to wrap the hockey stick I'm giving Jack." She got up to go, but on her way out, she paused, "You know, I have to give you credit, Hilary. Lots of people, if they'd saved all that money . . . Lots of people would spend it on themselves."

"Themselves?" Hilary straightened her glasses.

Angelica nodded. "You know that gadgety watch you like? The one in the window of Bennett Jewelers? A selfish person would keep her money to buy that."

Hilary watched Angelica vanish through the door. It would be nice to get that watch with the numerals that flashed and buttons that pushed and alarms that beeped and buzzed—

But I'd never do anything as selfish as that, thought Hilary. She straightened her glasses. I'm going to buy Jack the best aquarium there is. Even if I have to spend every penny.

"Uhf!" Hilary pulled down the piggy bank. It felt heavy. As heavy as the big dictionary at school. She sat down on the floor and shook the

bank. The money made a sound like gravel rattling on a beach when the tide went out. Jack had wanted an aquarium for as long as Hilary could remember. He'd be so surprised. She reached for the stopper in the pig's plump belly—

"Nnnh–nnnh–nnnh—"

Hilary stared.

The pig was sniffling. Tears glistened in its little eyes. Its pink ears that were just like Penny Wise's drooped. No longer did it show Hilary a smile, crooked or otherwise. Instead, its mouth drooped in a miserable upside-down U.

"What's wrong?" said Hilary.

"Nnnh-nnnh-nnnh—" The little pig rolled her eyes toward the stopper and kept sniffling.

Hilary said, "You don't want me to touch the stopper?"

"Nnnh-nnnhh-nnnhh—" Tears dribbled down the pig's face and splashed onto Hilary's lap.

"But I have to get my money. It'll only take a minute—"

"Nnnh-nnnhh-nnnhh—" The piglet screwed up its face, and the tears fell even faster.

Hilary couldn't stand to see the little pig so un-
happy, but she didn't know what to do. She sat
back on her heels. "If I leave the money alone, will
you stop crying?"

The pig looked at Hilary and gulped.

"Will you?"

The little pig nodded a grateful, teary nod.

The next day as she and her mother drove
downtown, Hilary slumped in her seat beside the
window and felt just awful. As she waited in

Cuff's Stationery Store while her mother chose cake candles and balloons, she fingered her empty pockets and sighed. Her feet dragged as she followed Mrs. Hummer into Castor's Bakery to pick up Jack's cake.

"If I do say so myself, it's a beauty," Mrs. Castor held open the box so Mrs. Hummer and Hilary could see.

The layer cake was topped with a hockey rink and thirteen players who held hockey-stick candles. The scoreboard said, HAPPY BIRTHDAY, JACK!!!

"Jack will love it," said Mrs. Hummer as she rested the box on Hilary's lap and climbed back into the car. She started the engine. "Are you sure you don't want to stop at the pet store?"

Hilary held the cake box on her lap and glumly shook her head. "I wanted to give Jack an aquarium, but my piggy bank cried so hard when I tried to take out the money, I couldn't do it. I'm giving Jack something else." She thought about the three battered old hockey pucks she had found, now wrapped and sitting on the desk in her room. They weren't as nice as an aquarium. But they hadn't cost anything, and that had made her piggy bank feel cheerful.

Mrs. Hummer gave Hilary a sideways look. "Are you sure it was your piggy bank who didn't want to spend the money?"

Hilary stared. "Who else would it be?"

Mrs. Hummer shook her head and turned the car homeward on Beech Street.

Hilary watched the town hall glide past her window, Bob's Pet & Hobby Shop, Bennett Jewelers. As they approached the bank, she peered out to

catch a glimpse of Penny Wise's calm, reassuring smile—

Hilary rubbed her eyes, straightened her glasses, and looked again.

It was true. The giant pig's familiar smile had vanished. Penny Wise's huge brow was furrowed. Her mouth tight. Her expression serious. As Hilary watched, she mouthed the single word: *Selfish!*

That night Hilary watched the rest of her family watch Jack open his presents. Except for Jack, everyone knew that Hilary had planned to get him an aquarium. Except for Jack, everyone knew that instead, she had wrapped three used pucks. As Jack tore off wrapping paper, Hilary thought, Angelica believes it was *my* idea not to spend the money. So do Mom and Dad. Even Penny Wise thinks I'm the one who acted selfishly. But it was that little pig!

Fortunately, Jack liked the battered old hockey pucks. Or at least he said he did. "I can use these

instead of new ones for practicing! These are already beaten up."

As Jack laid aside the pucks, Hilary heaved a sigh of relief and thought, The next time someone has a birthday, I'll do a better job of standing up to that little pig.

Hilary went back to saving. She saved nickles. She saved quarters. She saved her allowance and her snow-shoveling money. The pig got heavier and heavier. Its smile got wider and wider. But it stayed crooked.

"Angelica's right. It is sneaky." Jack ambled into Hilary's room, flopped down on her bed, and stared at the pig on the top bookshelf.

Hilary didn't agree that it was sneaky. But it was the day before Angelica's birthday, and she was too excited to argue. "I'm just about to take out my money. Tomorrow I'm going to get Angelica a canary!"

"A canary?" Jack looked interested.

Hilary nodded. "One to go with Do-Re. So she'll have a pair. When Dad goes to the bakery to pick up Angelica's birthday cake, he's going to take me to the pet shop to get it."

Jack looked doubtful. "Canaries cost a lot of money."

"I'll bet I've got enough. I've been saving for months. Want to help me count?"

Eeep—eeep—eeep! beeped Jack's wristwatch.

Hilary watched Jack press a button, glance at flashing numerals, and shake his head.

"Can't, Hilary. I have hockey practice. Plus, I'm giving Angelica a backpack, and I've still got to wrap it."

As Hilary watched, he pressed other buttons on his watch and stood up to go.

On his way out of her room, he paused, "I have to give you credit, Hilary. Lots of people, if they'd saved all that money, would spend it on themselves."

Hilary watched Jack and his wristwatch vanish

through the door. Themselves? It *would* be nice to own a watch like Jack's. One with buttons, alarms, and flashing numerals—

But I'd never do anything as selfish as that, thought Hilary. She straightened her glasses. I'm going to buy Angelica the chirpiest canary there is. Even if I have to spend every penny.

"Uhf!" Hilary pulled down the piggy bank. It felt heavy. As heavy as the iron frying pan in the kitchen. She sat down on the floor and shook the bank. The money made a sound like a load of gravel pouring out the back of a dump truck. Hilary reached for the stopper in the pig's plump belly—

"Rrrrgggh—"

Hilary stared.

The pig's small pink ears pointed straight back. Its usually curly tail pointed straight down. It stared at Hilary out of narrowed eyes.

"What's wrong?" said Hilary.

"Rrrrgggh—" The pig curled back its lip to bare a row of small, sharp teeth.

"But I have to take out the stopper to get the money—"

Clmppp!

Hilary jerked away her finger an instant before those small, sharp teeth snapped it. Her heart was pounding. Her arms and legs trembled as she sat back on her heels. "If I leave the money alone, will you calm down?"

The pig stared at Hilary and nodded a single fierce nod.

The next day as she and her father drove downtown, Hilary slumped in her seat beside the window and felt just awful. As they stood at the cash register in Stewart's Market while Mr. Hummer paid for milk and party napkins, she fingered her empty pockets and sighed. Her feet dragged as she followed him into Castor's Bakery.

"It's another beauty!" Mrs. Castor held open the box so Hilary and Mr. Hummer could see.

The layer cake was topped with a black-and-white dance floor. On it, fifteen tap dancers tapped. Each balanced a candle on his or her head, and the letters on the floor spelled out HAPPY BIRTHDAY, ANGELICA!

"Angelica will love it." Mr. Hummer rested the box on Hilary's lap and climbed back into the car.

He started the engine. "We've still got time to stop at the pet store. How about it?"

Hilary held the cake box and shook her head. "I wanted to give Angelica a canary, but my piggy bank got so angry when I tried to take out my money, I was afraid to do it. I'm giving Angelica something else." She thought about the two very old gold-and-silver glitter barrettes she had wrapped and left on the desk in her room. Since the day Clover got out of her cage and chewed them, those barrettes had more tooth marks than they had glitter. Two barrettes weren't as nice as a second canary. But they hadn't cost anything, and that had made Hilary's piggy bank calm down.

Mr. Hummer gave Hilary a sideways look. "Are you sure it was your piggy bank who didn't want you to spend the money?"

Hilary stared. "Who else would it be?"

Mr. Hummer shook his head and turned the car homeward on Beech Street.

Hilary watched the town hall glide past her window, Bob's Pet & Hobby Shop, Bennett Jewelers.

As they approached the bank, Hilary scrunched down in her seat. She didn't want Penny Wise to see her, but she couldn't resist peeking out the window to catch a glimpse—"Ohh!"

High on the roof, looking straight into the car at Hilary, stood Penny Wise. She didn't smile. She didn't frown. She shook her huge head with a look that said, "I am *very* disappointed in you."

That night as Angelica tore off wrapping paper, Hilary thought, Everyone thinks it was my idea not to spend any money. Even Penny Wise believes I'm the one who's selfish, but it isn't me. It's that little pig!

Luckily, Angelica liked the barrettes. Or at least she said she did. "I can use these when I ride my

bike after dark. If people don't see my headlight or reflectors, they'll see my glittery barrettes."

As Angelica laid aside the barrettes, Hilary made up her mind, thinking, The next time someone has a birthday, I'm going to stand up to that pig!

Hilary tried. She tried on Mother's Day when she wanted to buy Mrs. Hummer an ant farm. She tried on Father's Day when she wanted to buy Mr. Hummer a watercolor paint set. When she wanted to buy Clover a Gerbil Gymnasium for her birthday, Hilary tried again.

"Ouch!"

That night at dinner Hilary unwound the Band-Aid from her finger. "I stood up to that piggy bank today, and it bit me!"

Jack grabbed her finger, studied the little red marks, and pushed it away. "Gerbil nip."

"It was the pig!" said Hilary.

Angelica gulped her soup. "If I were Clover and you'd promised me a Gerbil Gymnasium, and then were too stingy to buy it. . . . Well, I'd nip you, too."

"The pig did it!" said Hilary.

Mr. Hummer coughed.

Mrs. Hummer straightened her place mat.

Angelica looked across the table to Jack and rolled her eyes.

"That little pig did it!" Hilary turned from one member of her family to another. Nobody looked convinced.

The following Friday on their way home from

the library, Hilary and Angelica noticed a sign in Bennett Jewelers' window:

They braked their bikes and got off to look.

Hilary stared through the window. There in the front row, on the dark blue satin display cloth, lay the chunky timepiece with the numerals that flashed, buttons that pushed, and alarms that beeped and buzzed. "If I could get the money out of my piggy bank, I'd buy you," whispered Hilary.

Angelica gave her a hard look. "Your piggy bank never let you take even a penny for presents. It would be pretty odd if it let you have the money for that watch."

Hilary shrugged. "My piggy bank has been difficult until now. But—"

Above Angelica's head, something moved. Something large and pink. It stood atop the bank roof across the street, and it was glaring at Hilary.

Don't do it, Hilary! Don't buy that watch.

Hilary swallowed hard. She straightened her glasses. Then she had a better idea and took them off. Instantly, Angelica's face softened to a fuzzy blur. So did Beech Street. So did the bank building. Even the large glaring something across the street blurred until it was no more than a cloud of soft pink.

Hilary had wanted that gadgety watch for as long as she could remember. She could imagine how the watch would feel on her wrist. She could imagine how it would look. She could imagine how everyone in school would turn to stare when her alarm beeped on the playground, during lunch, in the middle of a spelling test. The minute she and Angelica got home, she hurried to her room.

"Uhf!" Hilary pulled down the pig. It felt heavy. As heavy as her baby cousin Geoff. She sat down on the floor and shook the bank. The money made a sound like a car engine trying to start on an icy morning. It would have been nice to get Jack that

aquarium for his birthday; Angelica, the canary; Mrs. Hummer, the ant farm; Mr. Hummer, the watercolor set; and Clover, the Gerbil Gymnasium, but it wasn't Hilary's fault. She'd tried. The piggy bank just hadn't let her.

Slowly, she turned the bank over in her lap. She reached for the stopper in its plump belly.

The little pig didn't sniffle. It didn't snarl, nip, or bite. Instead, it lay calmly on its back. Its short stocky legs stuck straight up in the air.

"What do you know!" breathed Hilary. With trembling fingers she turned the stopper and pulled. With thumping heart she turned the bank upright.

Whsssssss! Coins poured onto the floor.

"What do you know!" repeated Hilary.

The little pig looked up at her and smiled its crooked smile.

Hilary counted her money. When she finished, she dumped her dominoes out of their red velveteen storage sack and poured the money inside.

The next morning she lugged the sack with her to the breakfast table.

Mrs. Hummer glanced up from her tea. "You'll need an armored car to carry all those savings downtown."

"Unh!" Hilary hefted the sack onto the table beside her place. She sat down and spread her napkin over her lap. "The jewelry store's not so far."

Mr. Hummer eyed Hilary's left wrist. Her sweater cuff was folded neatly back to leave a wide, bare space. "So you're really going to buy that watch?"

Before Hilary could answer, Angelica said, "How did you get your piggy bank to see reason?"

Hilary helped herself to a cranberry muffin and straightened her glasses. "I think that pig was tired of holding all this heavy money. It didn't cry, snarl, or put up any fight at all."

"Strange," said Mrs. Hummer.

"Most unusual," agreed Mr. Hummer.

Jack stared at Hilary. "I call it downright suspicious."

Hilary swallowed a bite of cranberry muffin and shrugged. "It's very *pig*-culiar!"

No one smiled.

Hilary tried to, but muffin crumbs made her lips stick to her teeth so that the smile came out—crooked.

"That one, there, in the front row." Hilary stood on the sidewalk in front of the jewelry store and pointed.

Inside the shop Mrs. Bennett reached into the display window where dozens of watches floated on a sea of dark blue satin.

Hilary put her finger to the glass. "It's the one right here. Not that one. The next—"

The morning sun burst through a covering of clouds. Instead of watches, Hilary saw the buildings across the street. Bob's Pet & Hobby Shop, Cuff's Stationery Store, Castor's Bakery—they were all reflected in the jewelry store window. Penny Wise Savings Bank, and on top of the bank roof—

"Is it this one?"

Hilary shielded her eyes and saw that Mrs. Bennett had fished her gadgety watch from the dark blue satin. As she stared, the watch's luminous numerals blinked and flashed even more brightly than she'd remembered. She shifted her heavy sack to get a better grip.

Hilary, don't do it!

Even with her eyes shielded against the reflection, there was no mistaking that voice.

You have better things to do with your money.

"Is this the one?" said Mrs. Bennett.

Hilary felt nervous, but the longer she gazed at that flashing, blinking watch, the more determined she was to have it.

You have gifts to get, promises to keep!

Hilary looked from Mrs. Bennett to the watch. She didn't know what to say. She wanted to do what was right, but at the same time, she wanted that watch so badly, the skin of her wrist itched.

Hilary!

Hilary caught her breath and stepped back from the window. "I'm sorry, Mrs. Bennett. I've changed my mind. I'm not going to buy a watch today."

"No?" Mrs. Bennett looked surprised, but she

only shrugged and returned the watch to its place in the display.

Hilary straightened her glasses. "I have other things to do with my money. I have gifts to get, promises to keep."

Mrs. Bennett glanced at Hilary, who was still staring into the window, and thought she was speaking to her. "That's fine, dear. No need to explain."

Hilary barely heard her. She was concentrating too hard on the giant pink face reflected in the jewelry store window. She was watching its ferocious scowl melt, as she spoke, into a kindly, understanding smile.

"So I lugged my money straight across the street to Bob's Pet & Hobby Shop, and I bought all this!" Hilary waved a hand to indicate everything on the kitchen table. Mrs. Hummer's ant farm. Mr. Hummer's watercolor paint set. Jack's aquarium. Angelica's canary, Ti-Do. And Clover's Gerbil Gymnasium.

Jack nudged Angelica. "Bob's Pet & Hobby sent their delivery van."

"I rode home in it," said Hilary.

From his perch on Angelica's finger, Ti-Do chirped, *"Tweeet!"*

"It's lucky for all of us that Penny Wise was on the job." Mrs. Hummer set her ant farm on the window sill.

Mr. Hummer tested the tip of his paintbrush and nodded. "Hilary's little bank turned out to be quite a big pig."

"I'll say." Jack sprinkled the aquarium water with fish food. "If I were Hilary, I'd take that greedy piglet back to the bank and trade it in for a lollipop."

Hilary unfolded the assembly directions for the Gerbil Gymnasium. "I've done something better than that. As soon as I got home, I took out my space explorer's transporter and beamed that selfish, sneaky pig straight to the Forgotten Planet. One way!"

Angelica rolled her eyes. "Hilary! I saw exactly how you 'beamed' it, and where."

"Wel-ll—" Hilary straightened her glasses. "Our garbage can was the closest I could get to outer space."

5 | Go, Fish!

Hilary pricked up her ears.

"I'll tell you what the difference is. She's not a little girl anymore. She's begun to act like a grown-up." Angelica's voice wafted from the living room down the hall to where Hilary sat on her bedroom floor playing Forbidden Planet with her space explorers.

"She *is* less daydreamy," said Mrs. Hummer's voice.

Hilary locked the space explorers into planet orbit and crept out of her bedroom and down the hallway so she could hear what everyone was saying.

"She's more organized. More practical," said Mr. Hummer's voice.

Jack's voice agreed. "You can talk to her as though she were a real person now, not a little kid."

Hilary's face felt warm. They were talking about her! The things they were saying about her were nice things. Her heart began to pound and a ticklish feeling filled her chest. She felt almost exactly

the way she did at school when she tried to talk to Dexter. She reached to straighten her glasses, and the interstellar space probe that had been hanging half in, half out of her pocket fell on the floor.

"Hilary, are you there?" called Mr. Hummer.

Hilary picked up the space probe and hurried down the hallway to the living room.

Her mother, father, Angelica, and Jack all looked up at her.

Mr. Hummer said, "We were just talking about you. Have you been out there long?"

Hilary caught sight of the newspaper lying on the coffee table and hurried to pick it up. "Not

long. I was looking for the newspaper. I need to write a paper after dinner for Monday's Current Events."

Mrs. Hummer smiled. "I think Angelica and Jack have other plans for the way you'll spend your Saturday evening."

"Plans?" Hilary looked at Angelica and Jack.

Jack said, "We're going to the roller rink, and we want you to come with us."

Hilary stared. The rink was where Angelica and Jack went on weekend evenings to meet their junior high school friends. They never invited Hilary to go along. In the past when she'd asked to join them, their answer had been one word. "No!"

Jack leaned forward. "Last week we saw Erin there with her big brother."

Angelica said, "Flip was there, too, and Tanasha's big sister Kranshi said they'd be there tonight. Also Dexter Small."

"Dexter?" said Hilary.

Mr. Hummer said, "You'd better take a bath before you go. You got pretty grimy playing Frisbee football in that muddy field across the street."

Angelica said, "We want to leave right after dinner, Hilary. If you're going to take a bath, you'd better do it now."

Hilary took clean clothes out of her dresser drawer. "I'll wear my new sweater, the red one with the reindeer," she said to Clover.

Clover was edging along the balance beam of her gymnasium and concentrating too hard to pay much attention to what Hilary said. *"Nffft-nffft-nffft—"*

Hilary hurried to the bathroom, closed the drain, and turned the tap. *Wssshhh*— Water gushed from the faucet into the tub.

Hilary thought, I can skate backward really well, and I can twirl pretty well. She imagined herself gliding and twirling around the center of the roller rink while Angelica and Jack, and all their friends gazed on in admiration.

If only I had some bubble bath, thought Hilary.

From the shelf that held shampoo, soap, and Hilary's faithful old rubber duck, Angelica's white-and-gold bottle of Foaming Bath Milk sparkled down at her.

She hurried back down the hall to ask if she could use just a little. As she neared the living room, she heard her mother's voice.

"She's stopped letting her imagination run wild."

Angelica said, "Since that day last month when she bought us those great gifts, have you noticed she hasn't run into even one mysterious character?"

"That's true," said Mr. Hummer.

"You're right," said Jack.

Hilary stopped short and searched her memory of the past few weeks. School. Dancing class. Playing at Erin's and at Dean's. Cleaning her room. Homework. Visiting Uncle Gary's and Aunt Deb's . . . She straightened her glasses. Her family was right. There'd been no troublemakers at all. Not one.

"Don't anyone even mention mysterious characters!" said Mr. Hummer's voice.

Mrs. Hummer said, "In time, maybe we'll all be able to forget they ever existed."

No more troublemakers? Hilary crept back along the hall the way she'd come.

Inside the bathroom, as water gushed and the rubber duck bobbed, Hilary waited to feel relieved, even excited. When nothing like that happened, she untied her shoes and thought, Good riddance. I hated being bothered by those pests! She pulled off her socks. They never did anything but get me into trouble! She yanked her T-shirt over her head.

Besides, if they were still pestering me, Angelica and Jack would never take me roller skating!

Wrmmm— The bath water had reached the splash drain.

Hilary reached for the tap and turned it off.

All the same . . . She sat on the edge of the tub. It wasn't that she'd *liked* being pestered. But the idea of never again meeting a strange character who appeared to her and to no one else— *That* left her feeling let down. On top of that, she was starting to feel a little nervous about going roller skating. What if Erin, Tanasha, and Dexter weren't at the rink? What if no one she knew was there and no one talked to her? What if she stepped onto the polished boards in front of all Angelica's and Jack's friends and—fell?

Splss!

Hilary felt a splattering of warm water on her back. She turned to see where it had come from and sprang away from the tub. "Ohhh!"

A triangular gray fin sliced through the bath water. Back and forth, back and forth, from one end of the tub to the other it sped. That fin connected underwater to a long gray form with a powerful tail, two cold eyes, and a mouthful of—

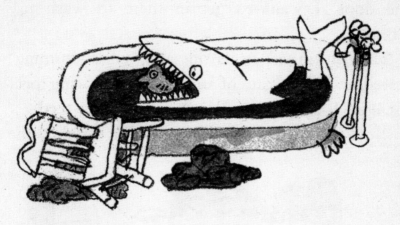

Smmmk!

The rubber duck disappeared below the surface of the water.

—gigantic, jagged teeth.

"Hilary?" Mrs. Hummer called through the bathroom door. "Hurry along. Dinner will be ready in fifteen minutes, and you've been in there for hours!"

"Coming." Hilary barely heard her. She was

staring at the powerful gray fish swimming back and forth, back and forth, in the bathtub.

"Hilary!" Jack rattled the doorknob. "Unlock the door. I want to get in there to wash my hands."

The fish turned on its side and, still swimming, stared at Hilary out of one small menacing eye. *Gnnnsh!* It snapped its dangerous-looking teeth.

"Just a minute," called Hilary. She watched the

gray fish flip its tail and continue its back and forth swimming. Ripples slapped the sides of the tub—*Wwwp—wwwp—wwwp—*

Mr. Hummer rapped on the door. "After all this time in the tub, we'll expect you to be squeaky clean!"

Hilary looked down at her grimy hands and dirt-streaked legs and thought, I'd better tell them. She started to open the door, but something stopped her. It wasn't *just* that no one would believe her. It wasn't *only* that by the time she got everyone to come look, the shark would certainly have disappeared. It wasn't even that Jack and Angelica would nudge each other and snicker, while Hilary's mother and father looked at one another and shook their heads—

"Hilary, if you don't come out, we're going to send in a search party!" called Mrs. Hummer.

The fish swam back and forth, back and forth.

Hilary couldn't take her eyes off it.

Who cared about spending Saturday evening with a bunch of big kids? she thought. She'd wanted Angelica and Jack to include her in things, to stop treating her like a baby, to treat her the way they used to before they went to junior high and started acting grown-up—but it hadn't occurred to her that to be one of them again, she'd be the one who'd have to change. She'd be the one who'd have to give up something.

"Hilary, this is getting silly. You can't stay in there forever," called Mr. Hummer.

Hilary stared at her fish. She didn't want to admit it, but her father was right. She couldn't stay in the bathroom forever, and she couldn't do little kid things forever, either. Once she started junior high, she'd not only be surrounded by big kids— She looked at the fish and sighed. "I'll be a big kid, too.

"Hilary!" yelled Jack.

The powerful, gray form moving through the bath water grew wavery, then shadowy—

Hilary turned to call, "I'm nearly done!"

When she looked back, the fish was gone.

"For a girl who's going to the roller rink this evening, you're being awfully quiet," said Mrs. Hummer.

Hilary looked up from her tuna casserole to see her whole family studying her. "I'm all right. That bath tired me out."

Mr. Hummer grinned. "I don't wonder. You were in that tub so long, I thought you must have melted."

"I thought you didn't want to go roller skating," said Angelica.

"I thought a killer whale must have gotten loose in the tub and eaten you," said Jack.

Hilary stopped chewing. Killer whale? All at once, she began to feel cheerful, excited—like her old self. "There wasn't any killer whale, but there *was* a—"

Jack nudged Angelica.

Mr. and Mrs. Hummer exchanged a look.

Mrs. Hummer prompted, "There was a—?"

Hilary straightened her glasses. In her mind's eye she saw the bathtub full of water, her yellow duck bobbing on the surface, and a darkish something that—the longer she looked—looked like nothing more than a shadow.

"There was a lot of dirt to get off my arms and legs. Grass stains, too. That's what took me so long."

"Well!" Mr. Hummer let out a deep breath and looked around the table at everyone else. "That's a relief."

Mrs. Hummer said, "You did a fine job. You look clean as a whistle."

Jack said, "For a minute, we were afraid you were going to say—"

"Jack!" Mrs. Hummer gave him a sharp look. "We weren't going to mention that, remember?"

Jack looked from Hilary to Mrs. Hummer. "But—"

Mr. Hummer changed the subject. "You'll look out for your sister this evening, won't you, Angelica?"

Angelica shrugged. "Hilary doesn't need looking out for. All our friends like her."

"And she skates really well," said Jack. "Last week on the sidewalk—"

Hilary smoothed her napkin in her lap and stopped listening. In her mind's eye she saw the roller rink. She saw herself in her new red sweater, gliding, twirling, and weaving in and out among Angelica's and Jack's friends, and her own. Everything about that picture looked grown-up, exciting, mysterious. As for the troublemakers—

"Hilary, are you ready to go?"

Hilary blinked, straightened her glasses, and stood. Ready is exactly what Hilary was.